APR 3 0 2022

NO LONGER PROPERTY OF
THE SEATTLE PUBLIC LIBRARY

P9-CKC-061

For my friend Jessixa.

Thank you so much to Jason T. Miles, Jesse liams-Hauser, Kevin Slota, Lydia Ortiz, Taylor Norman, Jennifer Laughran, the Bagleys, Sunny, Story, and Puppy.

Copyright © 2022 by Darin Shuler. All rights reserved. No part of this book may be reproduced in any form without written permission from the publisher.

Library of Congress Cataloging-in-Publication Data available.

ISBN 978-1-7972-0688-2

Manufactured in China.

MIX
Paper from responsible sources
FSC™ C008047
FSC
www.fsc.org

Design by Lydia Ortiz.
Typeset by Riza Cruz and Lydia Ortiz.

Typeset in Darin's Hand. The illustrations in this book were rendered in mixed media.

10 9 8 7 6 5 4 3 2 1

Chronicle Books LLC
680 Second Street
San Francisco, California 94107
www.chroniclekids.com

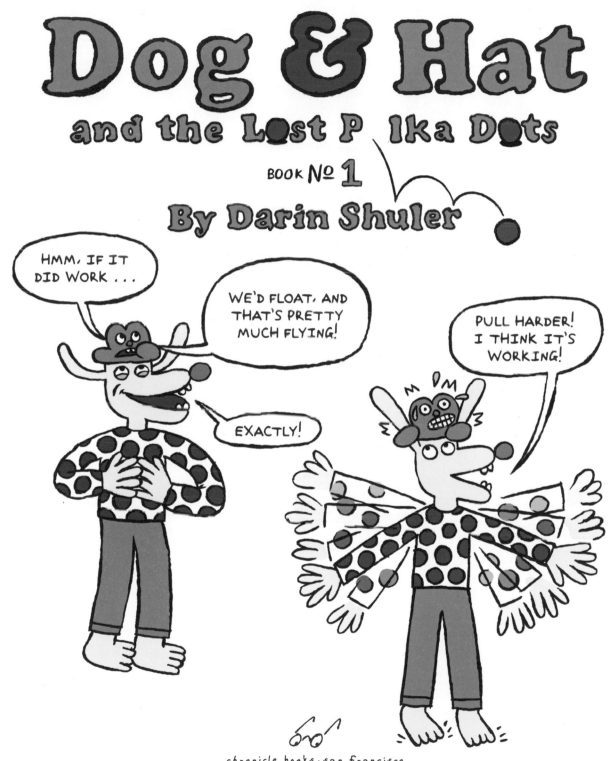

1

There They Go

2

You Can't Go
Underground Underprepared

3

Go with the Flow

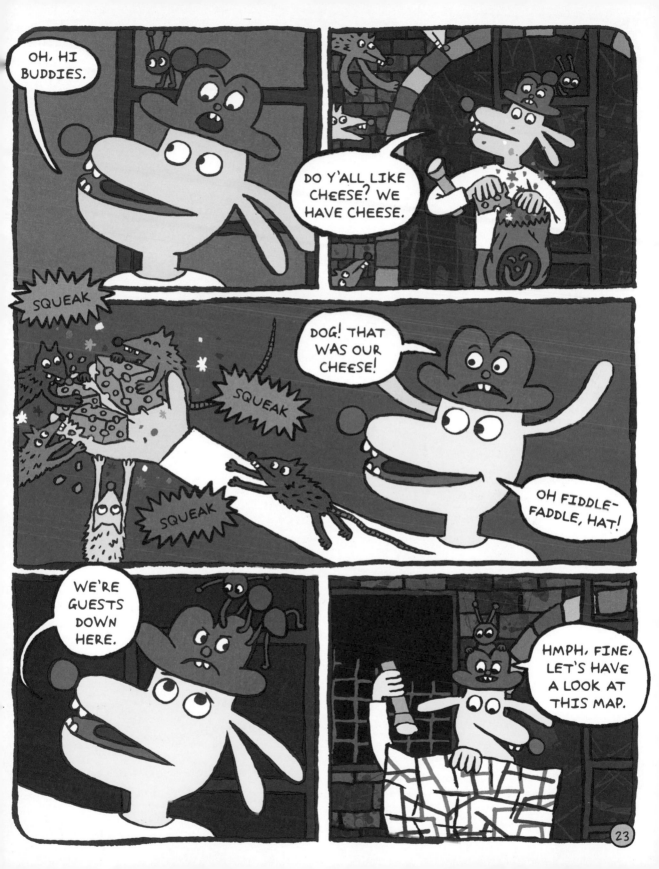

4

Heck or High Water

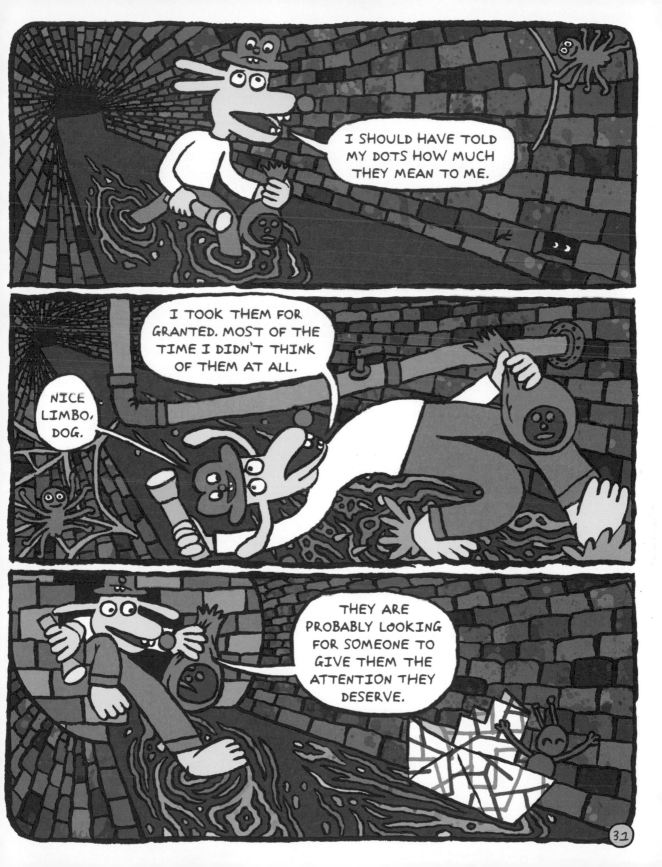

5

The Next Part of the Story

6

The Cure for
Polka Pox

7

Around the World
and Back Again